Katja Reider · Jutta Bücker

Rosalie and Truffle

Rosalie and Truffle

by Katja Reider
Illustrations by Jutta Bücker

Abrams Image

Library of Congress Cataloging-in-Publication Data

Reider, Katja.
[Rosalie und Truffel, Truffel und Rosalie. English]
Rosalie and Truffle / by Katja Reider ; illustrations by Jutta Bücker.
p. cm.
Summary: After meeting under an apple tree, two young pigs—Rosalie who dreams of love and Truffle who dreams of luck—
believe that their wishes have come true, until their friends offer them some questionable advice about relationships.
ISBN 0-8109-5984-4 (alk. paper)
[1. Pigs—Fiction. 2. Love—Fiction. 3. Self-acceptance—Fiction.]
I. Bücker, Jutta, ill. II. Title.

PZ7.R27375Ros 2005
[E]—dc22
2005015026

Production Manager: Jonathan Lopes
Designed and translated by Laura Lindgren

Copyright © Sanssouci im Carl Hanser Verlag, München – Wien 2004
Originally published in German as Rosalie und Trüffel, Trüffel und Rosalie.

English translation copyright © 2006 Harry N. Abrams, Inc.

Printed and bound in China
10 9 8 7 6 5 4 3 2 1

Published in 2006 by Abrams Image,
an imprint of Harry N. Abrams, Inc.
115 West 18th Street
New York, NY 10011
www.abramsbooks.com

Abrams is a subsidiary of LA MARTINIÈRE

A Story of Love

This is Rosalie.

This is Rosalie from the front.

This is Rosalie from the back.

And here she is from the side.

Rosalie loves to lie beneath the apple tree and dream.

Rosalie dreams of love.

"Don't you have anything better to do?"
Rosalie's father asks sometimes.
"You could learn French or practice ballet
or play a musical instrument . . ."

"If I had the kind of time you do," Rosalie's mother sighs.
"Oh, the the things I could do!"

"But I *am* doing something," says Rosalie. "I'm dreaming."

Later, Rosalie has two friends,

Lottie and Clara.

Lottie and Clara dream, too.

But only when nobody's looking.

Clara dreams of being famous.

Lottie dreams of being rich.

Not at all like Rosalie's dreams.
Rosalie dreams of love, especially now
that the apple tree is in full bloom.
Rosalie is on cloud nine. And she's not the only one.
For under the apple tree lies another pig.

"Truffle," Rosalie's bashful neighbor introduces himself.

"Rosalie," breathes Rosalie, blushing brightly.

"Now what?" whispers Truffle.

The rest is silence. And sighing.

Elated, Rosalie hurries off
to announce her joy to the world.
Oh, how happy Lottie and Clara will be!
But Rosalie is mistaken.
Her friends are worried.

Rosalie's in a tough spot.
Tough? Huh?
Rosalie doesn't understand.
Isn't it a dream come true?

Isn't everything glorious?

Lottie and Clara shake their heads.
What on earth can Rosalie be thinking,
getting involved with the first pig
to come along and lie beneath the apple tree!
That's no way to behave.

There's a whole world of pigs out there.
Rosalie should take a look around,
not go with the first pig to come along.
Rosalie is distressed.

Lottie and Clara know best —
Stop with the dreaming!
Rosalie should get to know a few pigs:

    nice pigs
      bad pigs
        poor pigs
          prickly pigs

In vain —

Rosalie dreams of Truffle.

Lottie and Clara sigh.

Rosalie is a hopeless case.

She believes this Truffle will love her forever, just the way she is.

With all the competition out there! Unthinkable! How naïve can you get?

Love is work. Passion is, too.

And Rosalie's going to have to give herself a good makeover:

Massage in the morning, workout in the afternoon,

power jogging in the evening,

nightly cucumber masks and yoga to combat stress.

There won't be a minute to spare for Truffle.

Such a shame, say Lottie and Clara,

but a woman must have her priorities.

Rosalie keeps quiet.

She makes the most of what she's got:

    a new hairstyle

       a new look

          a new outfit

"Fabulous!" Lottie shouts.

"Barely recognizable!" Clara exclaims.

And they're right.

Truffle drives right by Rosalie.

He doesn't even recognize her.

Rosalie is crushed.

"Forget him!" say her friends.
"All men are pigs.
 He doesn't really want you."

"Does too!" Rosalie cries. "That's just it —
 He wants me *really*."
 She cries her mascara off.
 She wallows in the dirt.
 She flees —
 Where to?

To the apple tree, of course.

The apples are ripe now.

How good they smell!

Rosalie is on cloud nine. And she's not the only one.

There beneath the apple tree is another pig.

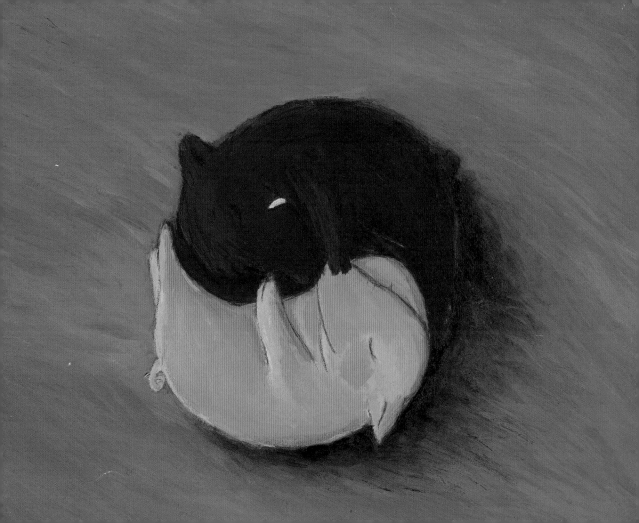

To the apple tree, of course.

The apples are ripe now.

How good they smell!

Truffle is on cloud nine. And he's not the only one.

There beneath the apple tree is another pig.

"But you were a nobody,"
say his friends.

"I was lucky," whispers Truffle.
He tussles his freshly styled hair
and flees —
Where to?

"So what?" say his friends.

"She wants an even better pig."

"She wants me the way I was!" cries Truffle.

And it's true.
Rosalie doesn't even look out the window
when Truffle drives by.
Doesn't she recognize him?
Has she forgotten him?

Truffle is devastated.

Because Truffle is playing the stock market,

training with his fitness guru,

souping up his little car — and himself.

"Completely transformed!" shouts Spike.

"Not a trace of the old Truffle!" exclaims Carlo.

Truffle does the best he can.

But there won't be any more time for Rosalie.

Truffle dreams of Rosalie.

Truffle is a hopeless case. Spike and Carlo sigh.

He believes this Rosalie will love him just the way he is.

But the competition!

Impossible!

A joke!

Women expect more from pigs:

Success, money, strength.

Passion — in proper doses.

Spike and Carlo know all about it.

In vain —

Spike and Carlo know best —
Stop with the dreaming!
Truffle's got to grow up and be a real pig!
There's a new delicacy on every corner:

    hot

       spicy

            sweet and sour

Truffle must sample them all!

Spike and Carlo shake their heads.
What's come over that Truffle,
getting snared by the very first sweet pig
lying under the apple tree!

Can Truffle possibly have fallen for her?
Let's hope not! After all, around every corner
await sweet new temptations, ripe and yours for the picking!
Truffle is dismayed.

Isn't it a dream come true?

Elated, Truffle hurries off
to announce his joy to the world.
Spike and Carlo are going to be amazed!
But Truffle is mistaken.
His friends are aghast.

What has Truffle gotten himself into?
Gotten into? Huh?
Truffle doesn't understand.
Isn't everything glorious?

"Truffle," he introduces himself, trembling.

"Rosalie," breathes his neighbor, blushing brightly.

"Now what?" whispers Truffle.

The rest is sighing. And bliss.

Carlo dreams about girls.

Not at all like Truffle's dreams.
Truffle dreams of being really lucky, especially now
that the apple tree is in full bloom.
Truffle is on cloud nine. And he's not the only one.
For under the apple tree another pig is dreaming, too!

Later, Truffle has two friends,
Spike and Carlo.
Spike and Carlo dream, too.
But only at night.

Spike dreams about chocolate cake.

"Isn't there *anything* you want to do?" asks Truffle's mother.
"You could work with your jigsaw or play hockey or
  do volunteer work for less fortunate little pigs!"

"When I was your age," Truffle's father chimes in,
"I was captain of the Wild Boars — the top scoring football team — and
  dreaming of being made quarterback."

"But I have dreams, too," says Truffle.

Truffle dreams a lot.
Best of all under the apple tree.
Truffle dreams of being really lucky.

This is Truffle dancing.

This is Truffle dreaming.

This is Truffle.

This is Truffle smiling.

A Story of Luck

Library of Congress Cataloging-in-Publication Data

Reider, Katja.
[Rosalie und Truffel, Truffel und Rosalie. English]
Rosalie and Truffle / by Katja Reider ; illustrations by Jutta Bücker.
p. cm.
Summary: After meeting under an apple tree, two young pigs—Rosalie who dreams of love and Truffle who dreams of luck—
believe that their wishes have come true, until their friends offer them some questionable advice about relationships.
ISBN 0-8109-5984-4 (alk. paper)
[1. Pigs—Fiction. 2. Love—Fiction. 3. Self-acceptance—Fiction.]
I. Bücker, Jutta, ill. II. Title.

PZ7.R27375Ros 2005
[E]—dc22
2005015026

Production Manager: Jonathan Lopes
Designed and translated by Laura Lindgren

Copyright © Sanssouci im Carl Hanser Verlag, München – Wien 2004
Originally published in German as *Rosalie und Trüffel, Trüffel und Rosalie.*

English translation copyright © 2006 Harry N. Abrams, Inc.

Printed and bound in China
10 9 8 7 6 5 4 3 2 1

IM▲GE

Published in 2006 by Abrams Image,
an imprint of Harry N. Abrams, Inc.
115 West 18th Street
New York, NY 10011
www.abramsbooks.com

Abrams is a subsidiary of LA MARTINIÈRE

Truffle and Rosalie

by Katja Reider
Illustrations by Jutta Bücker

Abrams Image

Truffle and Rosalie

Katja Reider · Jutta Bücker